For the ancestors.

Eromose

FINCHLEY, ENGLAND 1995

WHAT HAPPENED NEXT!?
DID THE OBA SURVIVE!?

HE HAD MANY QUEENS!

THEY JUST LET THEM TAKE THEIR STUFF?
HM.
COWARDS.

I BET THE OBA HAD MANY WIVES SO...

WHAT ABOUT THE QUEEN DADDY!
TELL US ABOUT THE QUEEN!

THERE WAS NO QUEEN, SILLY.

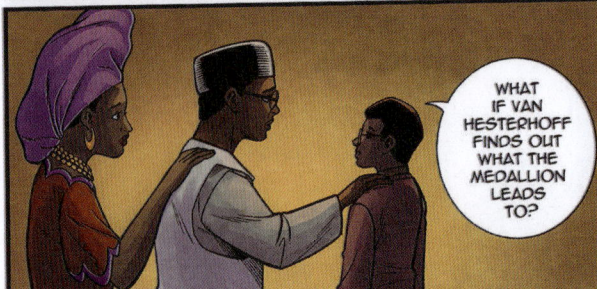

Episode 2
In The Name Of Our Fathers